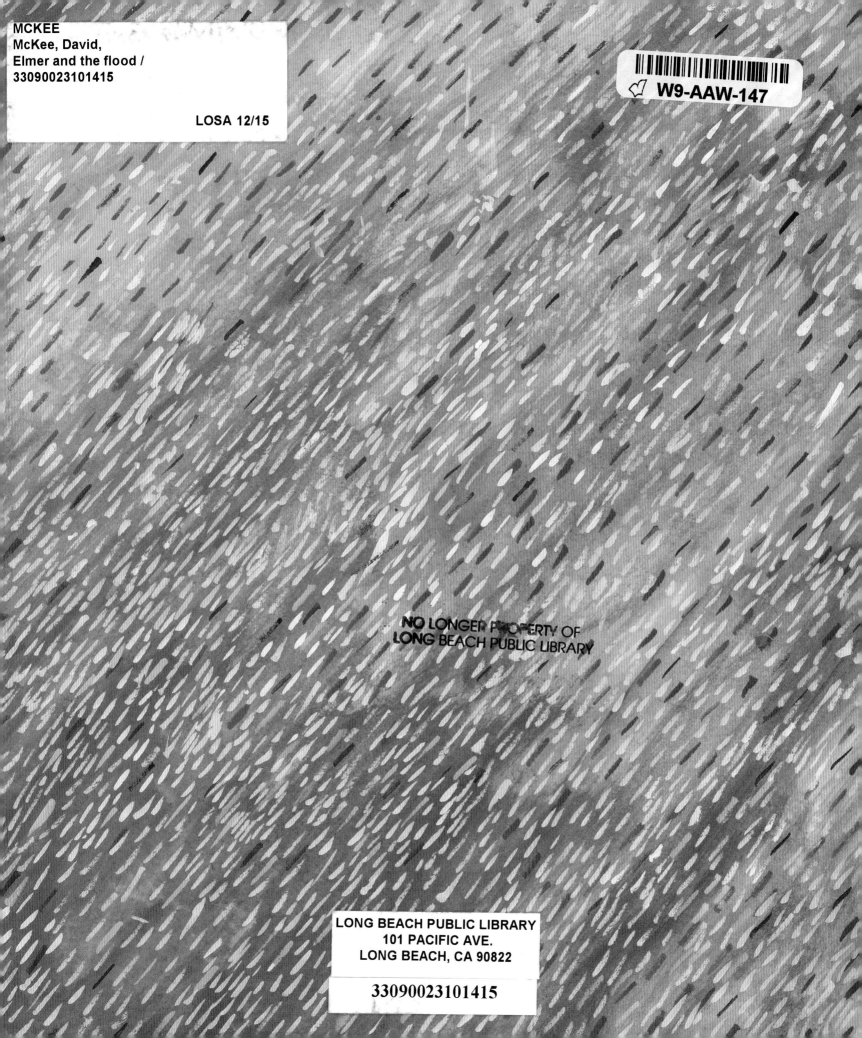

W9-AAW-147

Also by David McKee:

Elmer and Butterfly
Elmer and Rose
Elmer and Snake
Elmer and Super El
Elmer and the Big Bird
Elmer and the Birthday Quake
Elmer and the Hippos
Elmer and the Monster
Elmer and the Rainbow
Elmer and the Whales
Elmer's Christmas
Elmer's First Counting Book
Elmer's Opposites
Elmer's Special Day

American edition published in 2015 by Andersen Press USA,
an imprint of Andersen Press Ltd.
www.andersenpressusa.com

First published in Great Britain in 2015 by Andersen Press Ltd.,
20 Vauxhall Bridge Road, London SW1V 2SA.

Text and illustrations copyright © David McKee, 2015.

Distributed in the United States and Canada by
Lerner Publishing Group, Inc.
241 First Avenue North
Minneapolis, MN 55401 USA
For reading levels and more information, look up this title at www.lernerbooks.com.

Color separated in Switzerland by Photolitho AG, Zürich.
Printed and bound in Malaysia by Tien Wah Press.

Library of Congress Cataloging-in-Publication Data Available.
ISBN: 978-1-4677-9312-4
1-TWP-7/15/15

ELMER
and the FLOOD

David McKee

Andersen Press USA

Elmer, the patchwork elephant, was in a cave with
the rest of his herd. For days they'd been sheltering from
the torrential rain. Elmer had heard enough bad jokes and
complaints about the weather to last him a very long time.

"I need some peace and quiet," he said. "Rain or no rain,
I'm going for a walk."

It was already raining less and Elmer felt good to be outside. He passed other caves full of animals.

"Come inside, Elmer," they shouted. "It's raining!"
"I do believe you're right," said Elmer with a smile
and kept on walking.

Elmer headed for the river, but suddenly, where
there used to be grass and plants, there was water and
crocodiles. Large parts of the jungle were flooded.
"This is fun," said the crocodiles. "We've never been able
to swim here before."
"Make the most of it," said Elmer. "In a few days all of
this will be dry again."

Further along, Elmer met two worried-looking elephants.
"We haven't seen Young elephant since the rain began,"
said one. "I hope he hasn't been washed away."
"I'll keep a lookout for him," said Elmer.

Next he met some ducks.

"Lovely weather, Elmer," they said.

"For ducks," said Elmer.

"But we are ducks," they laughed. "By the way, the floods have made an island along there and one of your chaps is stuck on it."

"Thanks," said Elmer. "That must be Young."

Elmer soon found the island and there was Young.
He was overjoyed to see Elmer.
"Please can you rescue me?" Young said. "It's
lonely here and I miss the others."
"I'll get help," said Elmer. "Don't worry, I'll be
back soon."

The rain had stopped by the time Elmer arrived back at the cave. The elephants began to come out and Elmer explained the situation.

"What are we waiting for?" said the elephants excitedly.
"Come on!"

As the elephants hurried along, other animals joined them, happy to have some action after spending so long sheltering from the rain. They were all surprised by the flood water.

When Young saw the little parade arrive,
he danced for joy.
"Alright Elmer," said an elephant,
"what do you want us to do now?"

Elmer explained his plan. The monkeys brought creepers
to use like a rope and Elmer threw one end to Young.
"Pass it around a tree and throw it back," he said.

Young did as he was told.
"I hope you don't expect me to walk a tightrope, Elmer?"
he said rather worriedly.

They tied the ends of the rope to either end of a big log.
Elmer stood on the log, then the animals pulled on the
rope and Elmer was ferried across to the island.

He hopped off and Young took his place on the log. The animals carefully pulled him to safety. As Young arrived, an elephant whispered, "Let's trick Elmer. Untie the rope!"

"Oh dear Elmer," giggled one of the elephants. "The rope
has come off. How will you get back?"

"Good," chuckled Elmer. "That saves me doing it. I'll
be happy here until the flood waters go down. Finally
I can have a bit of peace and quiet. Bye!" he said.
"See you soon."